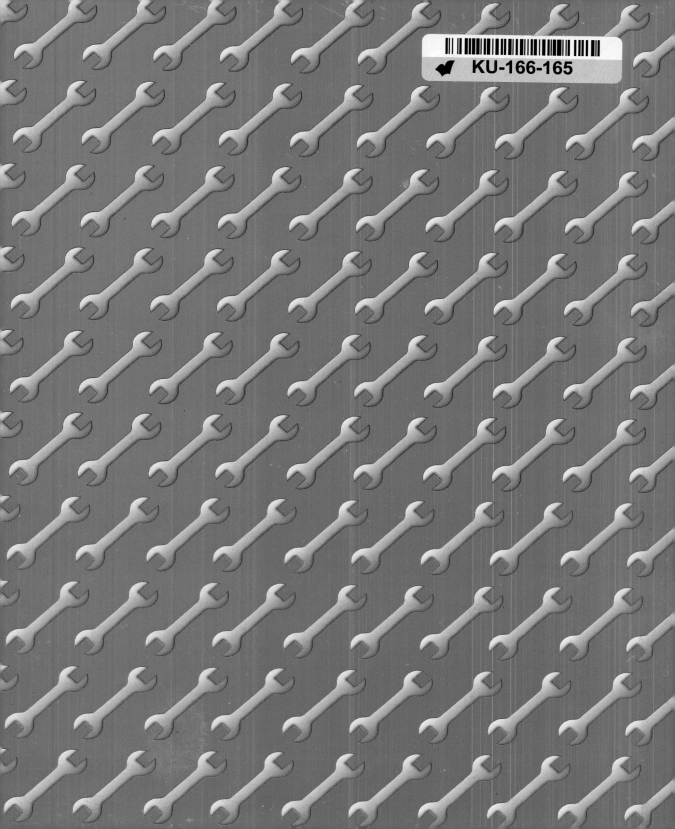

© 2001 Bookmart Limited

Published by
Armadillo Books
an imprint of
Bookmart Limited
Registered Number 2372865
Trading as Bookmart Limited
Desford Road
Enderby
Leicester
LE9 5AD

ISBN 1-90046-666-X

Produced for
Bookmart Limited by
Nicola Baxter
PO Box 215, Framingham Earl,
Norwich NR14 7UR

Designer: Amanda Hawkes

Printed in Indonesia

Starting to read – no trouble!

The troublesome truck in this story helps to make
sharing books at home successful and enjoyable.
The book can be used in several ways to help
beginning readers gain confidence.

You could start by reading the illustrated words
at the edge of each lefthand page with your
child. Have fun trying to spot the same words in
the story itself.

All the words on the righthand pages have already
been met on the facing page. Help your child to
read these by pointing out words and groups of
words already met.

Finally, all the illustrated words can be found
at the end of the book. Enjoy checking all the
words you can both read!

The Trouble with

Trucks

Written by Nicola Baxter · Illustrated by Geoff Ball

ARMADILLO

truck

driver

driver's mate

road

A big truck is rumbling down the road.

"Oh no! We're late!" says the driver, looking at his watch.

"Look out!" his mate cries.
"Keep your eyes on the road!"

"Sorry!" says the driver.
"Let's try this short cut."

"No! Keep on this road!"
says his mate.

lane

car

lady

bicycle

But it is too late. The driver turns into a lane.

The lane is very small.

The truck is very big.

Here comes a car.

Behind the car is a lady on a bicycle.

"We can't get past! Go back!" shouts the truck driver.

"No! You go back!" says the lady.

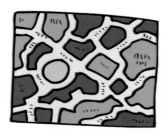

map

grass

Very slowly the truck goes back.

"No more short cuts!" says the driver's mate.

The truck stops. The driver and his mate get out. They spread a map on the grass.

factory

hill

"The factory is behind that hill," says the driver.

"No! It is behind **that** hill!"
says his mate.

workman

foreman

boss

lunch

At last the truck arrives at the factory.

"You're late!" says a workman. "I'll have to get the foreman."

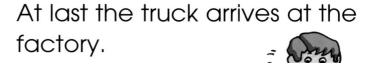

"You're late!" says the foreman. "I'll have to get the boss."

The boss is eating her lunch. She is not happy.

"You're late!" says the boss.

list

hand

dinner lady

hot pot

The boss goes back to her lunch. Now everyone is shouting.

"Back! Back!" yells the foreman, waving his list.

"Right hand down a bit!" shouts the workman.

"Look out!" cries a dinner lady. "Watch my hot pot!"

But the truck does not look out. The truck goes on backing.

The hot pot goes over everyone!

jacket

plates

lunchboxes

flasks

"Sorry!" says the driver.

"Sorry!" says the driver's mate.

"What about my jacket?" cries the foreman.

"What about my plates?" cries the dinner lady.

"What about our lunch?" cries the workman.

The driver and his mate hand over their lunchboxes and flasks.

"You can have **our** lunch," they say.

mess

mop

bucket

cap

The driver and his mate help to clean up the mess with a mop and a bucket.

At last they can set off again. But along the road, the driver takes off his cap and scratches his head.

"We've made a mistake," he says.

"Another one?" groans his mate.

"Yes, we forgot to unload the truck at the factory!"

"Oh no!" groans the foreman.
"Here comes that truck again!"

Picture dictionary

Now you can read these words!

bicycle

boss

bucket

cap

car

dinner lady

driver

driver's mate

factory

flasks

foreman

grass

hand

hill

hot pot

jacket

lady

lane

list

lunch

lunchboxes

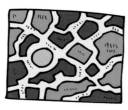

map

mess

mop

plates

road

workman

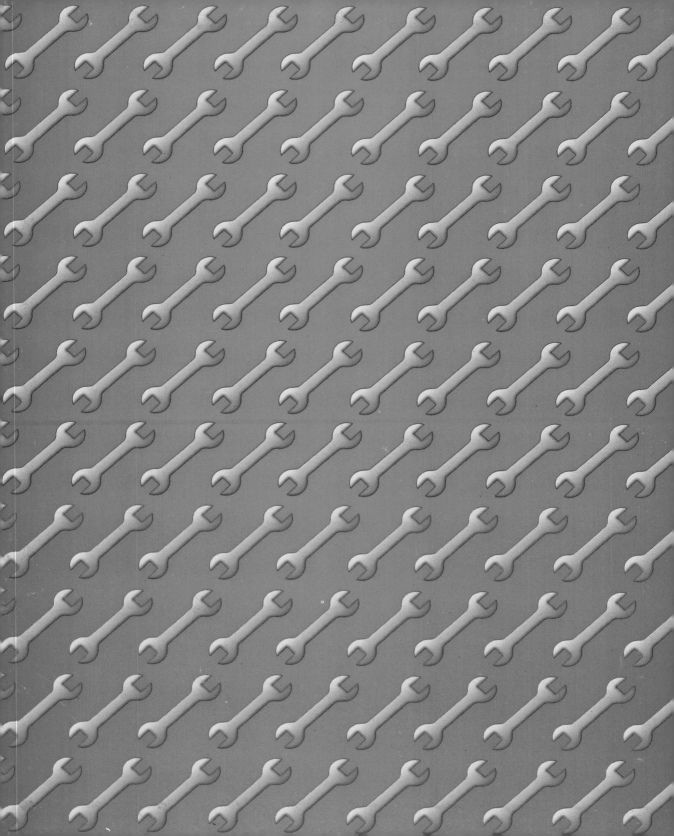